THE
HOLE IN
THE DIKE

Thanks to
Carol Klein
and the Westport Library,
Ina Micheels,
and
Dutch boys everywhere.

THE
HOLE IN THE DIKE

Retold by Norma Green
Pictures by Eric Carle

SCHOLASTIC INC.
New York Toronto London Auckland Sydney

A long time ago, a boy named Peter lived in Holland. He lived with his mother and father in a cottage next to a tulip field.

Peter loved to look at the old windmills turning slowly.

He loved to look at the sea.

In Holland, the land is very low, and the sea is very high. The land is kept safe and dry by high, strong walls called dikes.

One day Peter went to visit a friend who lived by the seaside.

As he started for home, he saw that the sun was setting and the sky was growing dark. "I must hurry or I shall be late for supper," said Peter.

"Take the short-cut along the top of the dike," his friend said.

They waved good-bye.

Peter wheeled his bike to the road on top of the dike. It had rained for several days, and the water looked higher than usual.

Peter thought, "It's lucky that the dikes are high and strong. Without these dikes, the land would be flooded and everything would be washed away."

Suddenly he heard a soft, gurgling noise. He saw a small stream of water trickling through a hole in the dike below.

Peter got off his bike to see what was wrong.

He couldn't believe his eyes. There in the big strong dike was a leak!

Peter slid down to the bottom of the dike. He put his finger in the hole to keep the water from coming through.

He looked around for help, but he could not see anyone on the road. He shouted. Maybe someone in the nearby field would hear him, he thought.

Only his echo answered. Everyone had gone home.

Peter knew that if he let the water leak through the hole in the dike, the hole would get bigger and bigger. Then the sea would come gushing through. The fields and the houses and the windmills would all be flooded.

Peter looked around for something to plug up the leak so he could go to the village for help.

He put a stone in the hole, then a stick. But the stone and the stick were washed away by the water.

Peter had to stay there alone.
He had to use all his strength
to keep the water out.
From time to time he called
for help. But no one heard him.

All night long Peter kept his finger in the dike.

His fingers grew cold and numb. He wanted to sleep,
but he couldn't give up.

At last, early in the morning, Peter heard a welcome sound. Someone was coming! It was the milk cart rumbling down the road.

Peter shouted for help. The milkman was surprised to hear someone near that road so early in the morning. He stopped and looked around.

"Help!!" Peter shouted. "Here I am, at the bottom of the dike. There's a leak in the dike. Help! Help!"

The man saw Peter and hurried down to him. Peter showed him the leak and the little stream of water coming through.

Peter asked the milkman to hurry to the village. "Tell

the people. Ask them to send some men to repair the dike right away!"

The milkman went as fast as he could. Peter had to stay with his finger in the dike.

At last the men from the village came. They set to work to repair the leak.

All the people thanked Peter. They carried him on their shoulders, shouting, "Make way for the hero of Holland! The brave boy who saved our land!"

But Peter did not think of himself as a hero. He had done what he thought was right. He was glad that he could do something for the country he loved so much.

A NOTE FROM THE AUTHOR

Mary Mapes Dodge, an American woman who had never been to Holland, told this story to her children, making it up as she went along. It was first published as a chapter in her book *Hans Brinker, or The Silver Skates*. That was more than a hundred years ago.

Over the years, the story became so famous that whenever visitors were in Holland, they would ask about the boy and the dike.

And so the Dutch people decided to put up a statue in a little

town called Spaarndam, and on the base they carved these words:

OPGEDRAGEN AAN ONZE JEUGD ALS
EEN HULDEBLIJK AAN DE KNAAP DIE HET
SYMBOOL WERD VAN DE EEUWIGDURENDE
STRIJD VAN NEDERLAND TEGEN HET WATER

DEDICATED TO OUR YOUTH TO HONOR THE
BOY WHO SYMBOLIZES THE PERPETUAL
STRUGGLE OF HOLLAND AGAINST THE WATER

ISBN 0-590-46146-X

12 11 10 9 8 7 6 5 4 3 2   3 4 5 6 7 8/9

Printed in the U.S.A.   09
First Scholastic printing, February 1993